COLOR ME THURSDAY!

Dear Betty,

Always The Best

Sincerely

Linda Neff

COLOR ME THURSDAY!

◆

Stories from Behind the Stylist's Chair

Frieda Newton

Illustrations by Michael Lobasz

iUniverse, Inc.
New York Lincoln Shanghai

COLOR ME THURSDAY!
Stories from Behind the Stylist's Chair

Copyright © 2007 by Frieda J. Newton

All rights reserved. No part of this book may be used or reproduced by any means, graphic, electronic, or mechanical, including photocopying, recording, taping or by any information storage retrieval system without the written permission of the publisher except in the case of brief quotations embodied in critical articles and reviews.

iUniverse books may be ordered through booksellers or by contacting:

iUniverse
2021 Pine Lake Road, Suite 100
Lincoln, NE 68512
www.iuniverse.com
1-800-Authors (1-800-288-4677)

Because of the dynamic nature of the Internet, any Web addresses or links contained in this book may have changed since publication and may no longer be valid.

This is a work of fiction. All of the characters, names, incidents, organizations, and dialogue in this novel are either the products of the author's imagination or are used fictitiously.

Michael Lobasz is an illustrator and designer. He currently resides in Connecticut. Please visit www.rocknoats.com if you're interested in contacting Michael or viewing more of his work.

ISBN: 978-0-595-43108-3 (pbk)
ISBN: 978-0-595-87450-7 (ebk)

Printed in the United States of America

INTRODUCTION

The following stories were inspired by a lifetime spent behind the stylist's chair. Many hours were spent among good friends and bad hair days, funny co-workers and cranky children, hard to please customers and the joy of "The Perfect Cut". If it happened in a salon or hair dresser's chair, under a dryer or in a tanning booth, I've probably done it, or seen it happen. After all this time and all these unusual and interesting events, I felt it was time to put pen to paper and bring some of those tales to the world. Hopefully they will be as entertaining for you to read as they were for me to recall and reminisce on my life behind the chair.

COWLICKS

Cowlicks have always fascinated me. These are the crazy hair problems where the top of your head looks like Dennis the Menace. Over the years I have discovered that 9 times out of 10 times, the more cowlicks the person has, the more likely this person will be a world traveler. Is it a coincidence? Perhaps, but check your head for cowlicks and see if you fit the profile. Perhaps you might have a wonderful trip in your future.

FROM GOLD TO ORANGE

I have one customer with a very strange quirk. For some unknown reason, for which I am sure I will never understand, whenever I color her hair, she leaves the salon looking and feeling great. However, at her next appointment her hair has mysteriously turned an orange color. It's easy to tell by this mysterious change in hair color that someone, if not she, had applied peroxide to her hair.

HAIR SPRAY

You know this client; she just wants a little more hairspray. You get the style you wanted and the spray to finish, but the client says, "I need more spray!" So you use more and then she says, "Now I need freeze spray!" Now she claims that you forgot to spray her bangs. Okay. So you spray her again. Now I can't even find her under all that spray. I'm choking on the huge cloud of hairspray. Finally, the spray settles and I am convinced that her hair won't move for a week. It may even make her head bounce off her pillow, but she loves it! Until, of course, the following week when we start the process all over again. "More hairspray please!!"

EXERCISE ROLLER MACHINE

The exercise section of the salon has a roller machine that breaks down the cellulite on your legs and buttocks. I have a few customers who, when they got off the machine, moaned, groaned, and said that it was better than their husbands.

TRIM MY HAIR

Just a trim, I mean less than an inch. You are starting your haircut, then she spins around and says let me see how much your cutting off. She is confident with my styling abilities, but she's not sure if I ever attended a math class. As if I don't know what an inch is. We finally got through the inch haircut and she loved it. It was just what she wanted. Why do I feel as if I did four hours work? I guess it was all the mathematics!

GREEN HAIR

What hairstylist has never heard the question, "This won't turn my hair green will it? I never thought it would happen to me but it did. Yes indeed. I was distracted when reaching for my hair colors where by I mixed the wrong colors together. There is no way of knowing for at least ten to fifteen minutes what color you have created. The timer bell went off and I returned to check her color and realized there had been a terrible mistake. She had bright green hair! What's next you ask? Never let them see you PANIC! Calmly, I told my client that the color shade was not quite right for her, where upon, I reapplied another color.

The timer bell went off for the second time, and this time the results were perfect. She absolutely loved it. Finally my heart rate started to return to normal!

MISSION: IMPOSSIBLE

A young lady entered my salon, and asked if she could get a knot removed from her hair along with a shampoo. I replied, "No problem!" Boy was I wrong! For hours my staff and I worked on this lady's hair trying to remove this knot the size of a golf ball, and just as hard. There was no way this knot was moving. There was one alternative. You got it! The scissors came out, and away I cut, a new style was created for her that she could handle herself. Weeks had gone by and this lady appeared in the salon again with yet another knot.

EYE BROWS AND EYE BROW PENCIL

Waxing eye brows can be very tricky when you are just learning. Or, being rushed, you can wax too thin, leave holes, or remove the entire brow. Thank goodness for eye brow pencil. (Of course, you will inevitably get the client who says they are not thin enough.)

I WANT MY HAIR LONG

I had been cutting her hair short for many years. I had always tried to get her to change her hairstyle, but she always wanted to keep it the same. One day she finally decided it was time for a change. Hallelujah! She had decided to let it grow a little longer. I was delighted and welcomed the change. Not one week had passed, and she couldn't stand her hair growing any longer. Yes, it had grown an entire quarter of an inch. She is a typical type of person who wants to change their hairstyle, but they never can bring themselves to do it.

PROM NIGHT

The prom has always been a big night. Girls make their hair appointments early for the big event. Every year we hear, "I want something different other than wearing my hair straight down. I would love a lot of height and fullness with curls or wrap my hair up high, but please no gel, no teasing, and no hair spray. By the way it has to last all night!" Yeah! Right!

THE GRUMPY CO-WORKER

Have you ever had this happen to you? You come into the salon bright and smiling, ready to take on the challenges of the new day and then you hit that wall; that wall known as the grumpy-co-worker. No matter how hard you try, you cannot get a smile or a kind word out of this miserable individual. My mother warned me that I would have days like this; I just didn't expect it every day.

PRETTY BUBBLES IN HER HAIR

While in the process of styling a client's hair, I am usually reaching for whatever wave set bottles, lotions or gels I need to use. However with this particular client I was styling, I could tell that something was different about the texture of her hair. It felt very heavy, as if it had a lot of body. I double-checked my bottles to see if I had made a mistake, because it didn't feel quite right to me. To my surprise I was applying shampoo and not gel back into her hair. The following week this client asked me to use the same gel that I had used the previous week. I could not believe what I was hearing! She told me she loved the way her hair looked and felt. Little did she know that all week I lived in fear that it would rain and her head would turn into a bubble bath making pretty bubbles in the air.

THE FUNNY PHONE CALL

For years I have received obscene telephone calls and a husband of one of my long time employee's is always fooling around on the phone. I answered the phone as usual and this guy starts up with the typical obscene questions. I think it's him, so I started to joke around and answer his questions. We were going back and forth for a while. Just as the caller was getting more personal the salon door opens and my employee's husband comes walking through the door. I got so taken aback that I just started to laugh realizing that I had just had this conversation with an entirely different person. I hung up the phone. I immediately had to explain to everyone what had just occurred. We all had a hard laugh and still laugh about that phone call years later.

THE EXHIBITIONIST

Every salon has one. That particular client with all her unwarranted antics who has to show you everything they have. And there she is ... our favorite tanning client that loves to lift her skirt high in the air to show everyone her thighs. After she disrobes, she loves to run around the salon looking for anyone who will assist her in applying her tanning lotion. Why does she think this is necessary?

IT'S ONLY A DREAM

A customer of mine once told me of a nightmare she had. It was about me. In her dream she was chasing me, trying to stab me with a knife. I'm so glad we were good friends, because if she hadn't been who knows how she really felt. Could it have been blamed on a bad haircut?

ELEPHANT MAN

Every year he makes his waxing appointment just in time for his annual Halloween party. Can you guess what his costume is? You got it. He goes to his party as an elephant. Need I say more about his waxing appointment? I never thought I would have an elephant in my salon.

CAN'T HEAR!

While blowing out my customer's hair, I noticed he was trying to converse with me. Immediately I could tell he was becoming agitated and annoyed as I wasn't replying back. I finally put down my blow dryer and simply explained to him that I could not hear him talking because I had a blow dryer in my ear.

MOMMY'S LITTLE HELPER

My daughter always spent time with me at my salon. She was learning to become an entrepreneur at the early age of four. As I was busy working on clients all day long, she would keep herself busy by cleaning up, stocking the shelves and pretending to mark the retail merchandise. Much to my surprise, one afternoon she really did change all my original prices on the retail items that were on the shelves. She had marked them lower than my own cost to buy them. Oooooops!!! Thank goodness she didn't put up a sale sign.

THE FASHION SHOW

You know the one we all know, the same person who in my case walks into the salon "dressed to kill" very lovely—but that's not enough. The first words out of her mouth are, "I feel so fat today. You reply, no not at all, you look very good. She replies, "I feel fat and I feel like I'm not put together, I think I gained a half of a pound. I just heard this the day before and the day before that. It's really funny because I know she is on a fishing mission to get a compliment.

BUSINESS NEVER STOPS

My business had become so successful I needed to move the salon to a larger location. It was a family affair trying to get the boxes unpacked while my son put down the last remaining tiles on the floor. I was in and out of the salon carrying in boxes of supplies and equipment when a woman approached me on the sidewalk. She needed a waxing service. She explained to me that she had an emergency and begged me to please help her out. Her plea worked. She and I pulled the waxing table off the sidewalk and into the salon, around everyone who was busy working to finish the final touches of the new salon. We found a convenient spot to wax her eyebrows between some retail boxes. She was so grateful that she has continued to be a loyal customer ever since.

CLOROX

This is the dirty customer. I needed to use Clorox bleach to wash my hands after doing her hair. It took me three days washing with the bleach to get rid of the odor. Just call me Mrs. Clean!

OCTOBER

We all know what October means. It is the time of year when all elementary students return for their second haircuts. Along with them, they bring their little friends too: the dreaded HEAD LICE. Every October for almost 40 years, I go through the same ritual with special shampoos and tiny combs. This has undoubtedly been the most predictable problem I have faced with my clients. So bring 'em on. No problem. This is just one of nature's little pests that we can always count on seeing in October.

PEOPLE ARE STRANGE AND FUNNY

Exercise in my salon was pay as you go or sign up for a 3 month special. After 3 months you could sign up for 3 more. One client decided to get into my files and write in that she joined up for an additional 3 months. When I confronted her about this, she said she paid someone else—"Oh, no, it was my grandmother who paid for me." (Poor Grandma) I guess it was becoming too uncomfortable trying to get away with her deception, so she finally decided to move on!

THE TWINS AND THE HAIRCOLOR SWITCH

Early Saturday mornings the twins make their color appointment. It's not unusual for me to mix two colors at the same time. I seated the twins next to each other, as I would apply their colors together. I sat one twin on my right side and the other on my left. I quickly returned with their colors. One twin is slightly darker than the other. So as to not confuse the colors I purposely sat the twins the way I did. I applied their hair colors and waited for their allotted time to pass before shampooing them. After thirty minutes I shampooed one of the twins, and to my amazement her hair color was much too dark. I shampooed the other and her hair was much to light. I was baffled and asked the twins if they had moved from their chairs. They both said, "Yes, we got up for a cup of coffee and switched our seats."

YELLOW PAGE DILEMMA

In this business, we run into customers who do not keep their appointments, these people are called "no-shows" … One year I experienced an abundance of "no-shows," more than would be considered normal. New clients were scheduled for appointments, but they were not keeping them. As it turned out, I found out that a new telephone directory for the town was delivered with a misprint of my salon address. What was even worse is that the address belonged to a local competitor. All of my new customers were ending up at the other salon. Unfortunately, I had to live with this confusion until the following year when the new telephone books were reprinted.

CINDERELLA AND THE BALL

The big moment had arrived amid blaring trumpets and glittering lights. The guests were arriving in their finest attire, and I felt like Cinderella at the ball. The wine was chilled and the food was abundant. This had been a moment I had waited for all my life, the grand opening of my own business. One of the finest hair salons this town had ever seen. It was New York chic! It was a great opening with the support of all my family, friends and employees. However, when the last of my guests departed I was totally alone. The floors of my salon were gleaming when we started the evening, now they were badly marked and dirty from the festivities. Cinderella rolled up her sleeves, knowing full well that the party had ended, and the palace must be ready to receive new guests in the morning. With a rag mop in my hand, I looked at myself in the mirror and said, "I don't believe this ..." I had no choice but to get down on my hands and knees in my beautiful dress and scrub the floors clean. I mopped and scrubbed the entire salon. And before leaving, I looked back at my work and said, "I did it! What a proud moment for me.

A SMALL SALON MYSTERY

The staff and I could never figure out how two oily handprints; waist high, fingers pointed upward came to be pressed into the newly painted massage room wall. There were many theories put forward, with much laughter. What do you think?

THE CHILD SLIDER

Have you ever had a child who just won't sit still in the chair? I had a boy who was fidgeting in my styling chair, so I thought to use a booster chair to keep him safer and perhaps a little more controlled. I put the booster chair on my chair and sat him down comfortably. It was a simple haircut. Or at least I thought it was. Every time I went for his head he was gone. I grabbed him by the collar each time to pull him back up. I only turned away for a moment to grab a clip when he slid out of the booster chair down through the back of my styling chair and onto the floor. So, I decided to join him on the floor where I finished his haircut.

CHILD'S HAIRCUT

Your first child's haircut is one you will never forget. The child was up and down, never sitting still. He zigged while I zagged the entire time and inevitably in the process I cut a small slice off his ear. I was so upset that I couldn't finish the haircut, even though the mother appeared not to be the least concerned. She blamed her son and not me, however the blood was flowing and it would not stop. I was a wreck! My boss, at the time said I had to finish the cut so that I would not be afraid for my next child's haircut. Very reminiscent of when you get thrown from a horse, you have to get right back on!

THE CUTTING SMOCK

It was a typical Saturday morning. The salon was jumping, and everyone wanted his or her hair cut yesterday. My customer handed me her gift certificate before her haircut. She went into the back to change into a cutting smock. I could detect that this client was very preoccupied with something. After her haircut she left. I thought she went to change back into her clothes. However, as it turned out, she completely forgot to change. She got all the way home before she had realized she still had the smock on.

THE LUCKY DIAMOND

It was closing time when one of my employees suddenly realized her diamond was missing from her ring. We all came to her aid and covered every square inch of the salon looking for it. We looked high and low, over and under, in and out of everything we could think of. We looked through every trashcan full of hair, under every towel. Looking for this diamond was like looking for a needle in a haystack. We were determined to find it. No one was going to give up the search because we believed in luck. One of my employees happened to move a brush holder and something shiny caught her eye. Lo and behold! There it was, her lucky diamond.

DINNER THEATER

It was a low budget musical for a local but famous dinner theater. The production of Annie was quite an undertaking. The director expected me to purchase thirty wigs with four hundred dollars. I knew going into this that I would have trouble, with a capital T. Please keep in mind that we were not working with the best products for the money allotted to purchase these wigs. My staff and I worked for days and days trying to place finger waves and curls on all the wigs. When dress rehearsal time came, guess what happened? The damn wigs were too small. After all that time and effort, the wigs lay on top of their heads. They looked ridiculous. It was funny! I got out the scissors and did what any professional would do, I improvised and cut the seams, stretched the wigs as hard as I could, and bobby pined them all on tight. A perfect fit. And as we all know, the show must go on!

DIRTY TOWELS AND FLYING END PAPERS

End papers are used for wrapping the ends of the hair to put on a roller or rod. I had my own washer and dryer in the salon, so the washing of the towels was done there in the salon. By accident, one day 1,000 end papers fell into the washer along with the towels. They went unnoticed, and they all went into the dryer. When removing the dry towels from the dryer, 1,000 pieces of paper flew all over the room. We were all shocked and surprised, and laughed when we saw the floor covered with end papers. What a mess!

THE DOUBLE GIFT CERTIFICATE

A gentleman came into the salon to purchase two gift certificates. He openly admitted that one certificate was for his wife and the other gift certificate was for his girlfriend. I had to admit, I always did wonder if the women knew each other.

They did both use their gift certificates, but fortunately for him, not at the same time.

DOUBLE CHARGE

You know the type, she flew into the salon without a booked appointment and started demanding to have her hair washed and styled immediately. I was going to handle this appointment personally. I was taking her back to the shampoo bowl to get her hair shampooed when she started to complain about the shampoo I was going to be using. She said, she didn't want any "shit" on her hair. Knowing that we only used professional products, I took her insults with a smile. I knew right then I didn't need to have this woman come back. She complained all the way through the entire service. I bit the bullet as any professional would, until the service was completed. Now it was my turn, with a really big smile, I double charged her knowing she would be unhappy, never to return. She made her exit in a huff. Instinctively I knew she would be back to complain about the price I had charged her. And on cue, she reentered that salon complained again that she did not like her shampoo, so I offered to shampoo her again knowing that really wasn't the problem. She refused to be shampooed again, and made another major exit for the second time running to her car, which she had kept running in the parking lot when she came back in. She was so flustered when she got back to her car, she attempted to start it again and it made a terrible noise. She floored the gas and sped out of the parking lot. She was miserable when she left, but than again she was miserable when she came in. You just can't please them all.

HOT AND COLD WATER

I have had days at the salon when I battled with the water temperature. Either the water was extremely hot or it was extremely cold. You could never get the water temperature just right for some people. You try and try, but somehow you can never satisfy them. When rinsing one customer's hair, the water temperature turned frigid. She jumped up and the water went running down her back, now she was soaked. Oooooops. Has this ever happened to you?

THE FAST SWITCH

"You say you want what?" She had scheduled an appointment for a hair color. I applied the entire color to her hair and set the timer bell for 30 minutes. After 10 minutes had passed, she mentioned that her appointment was for a permanent wave, NOT a hair color. I was shocked as I looked at her and said, "Give me a moment; I'm going to need it!" I immediately checked the appointment book and saw that she was down for a hair color, and not a permanent wave. I shampooed her hair color off and proceeded to give her what she asked for. The customer is always right.

WHERE ARE MY GLASSES

You are having a creative day, because no matter what you are creating it comes out fabulous. I was creating a new hairstyle, and she was unresponsive. I couldn't quite understand why she wasn't reacting to this great new style that made her look ten years younger. I asked her if there was a problem with her new hairstyle, and she replied, "I don't know, I can't see without my glasses."

THE FAMOUS

I received a phone call at the salon from a secretary of a famous singer, who lives in the area. She requested either me, or could I send one of my employee's to the singer's home to pierce his famous actress girlfriend's ears. They were attending a formal black tie event at the White House that evening with President Clinton and the First Lady. I, unfortunately, was glued to the salon all day and couldn't get away. I truly would have enjoyed meeting these famous people that I have admired from afar throughout their careers. My employee arrived at his home, and was pleasantly surprised to be met at the front door by the singer's girlfriend. She quickly guided her to the master bedroom, which was filled with fresh flowers. Much to her amazement she was thrilled when the famous singer entered the room and introduced himself to her and asked if she needed anything. My employee's head was swooning because this singing star was of great acclaim. The chance to meet him and her was a once in a lifetime occurrence. Being a professional with many years under her belt, she quickly went to work preparing to pierce the young actress's ears, which was a gift from her boyfriend. Needless to say, it was not easy for my employee to get through the next half-hour without being star struck, but she made it. Upon leaving, she was again pleasantly surprised to find that the famous singer was as good a tipper as he was a singer. I'm just sorry I had to miss that house call.

COLOR ME THURSDAY

The hair colored appointment was made for Tuesday at 11:00, and then changed to Wednesday at 2:00. The customer called again and asked, "Could you just color me Thursday? "No problem at all!" I hung up the telephone knowing I would never see or hear from her again. Just an educated guess, I suppose.

THE DUCK

Every week, same time, same place, in comes a nice elderly woman, who has put her boots on the wrong feet. As she walked through the salon her right foot goes far left and her left foot goes far right, making her look like waddling duck.

INCENSE

A new client walked through the door of the salon holding candles and incense in her left hand and matches in her right hand. Before I had a chance to ask her what she was doing, she lit the incense and the candles and placed them all around the chair she would be sitting in. She explained to me she was getting rid of any evil sprits that might be present before letting me start on her hair. I had to ask myself if this lady was for real.

DO IT YOURSELF?

Did you really do this to yourself?

LET'S DO THE TWIST

The salon was buzzing and spring had sprung. The stereo was pumping out 50's songs and everyone was in a great mood. I was shampooing my customer along side of the other two shampoo girls. Our customers had their heads back and their eyes closed. Chubby Checker's The Twist was blaring through the salon. I just couldn't help myself ... I got in the groove and started to twist to Chubby while shampooing my client. I looked over at the other girls and they were dancing too! Looking at each other, not saying a word, we just kept dancing and laughing without our customers realizing that we were twisting away behind them. When I looked down at the customers, their feet were keeping time with the music. We were all groovin'. You can't keep a good song down. Music is so good for the soul!

THE BELLE OF THE BALL

He came into the salon and told me that he was attending a Ball. The party meant a lot to him and he wanted to look great. He bought every service he needed to in order to get ready for the Ball. He started with waxing his legs, arms, and his back. Off to the facial room and then he went for his massage. Next, he soaked his feet for his pedicure and ate his lunch at the manicure table while we applied fake nails painted bright red; a really nice color choice. Next his hair was shampooed before his makeup was applied. His lips were painted red to match his nail polish. Before, placing him under the dryer I asked him to change back into his clothes. He came back out in a beautiful, long, black gown down to his ankles, where you could see his choice of pantyhose and matching heels. He sat under the dryer where his last coat of polish was applied and drying. His hair was styled to float over his shoulders. Now all finished, I have to say; he was going to be the Belle of the Ball.

KIDS!

I love kids. One of my favorite clients happened to be a four-year-old boy. He was so enjoyable to talk to. As I cut his hair, we conversed about his garden. We talked about his tomatoes, carrots, lettuce and pumpkins he was raising for Halloween. He explained to me how and when he planted the seeds, and told me that when he came back for another haircut he would bring me something that he grew from his garden. Sure enough, for his next appointment he comes in carrying a little brown bag filled with tomatoes and carrots for me. He honored his promise to me. What a kid! This little boy is going far with such a great outlook on life!

PARENTS DON'T ASK

Over the years I have seen many changes with my child clients. Years ago a child was just brought into the salon and got his or her haircut. The child wasn't asked; their hair was just done. These days a child is "asked" if he or she would like a haircut. You do know, if you ask the question you will get an answer. NO! NO! NO! (Not the answer you wanted to hear however.) Now the kids are crying, kicking and screaming. What happens next is they are bribed with cookies, ice cream, candy or even a special surprise at their favorite store. It seems the louder they scream, the bigger the candy promised! I'm not sure; do they make a five-pound gumdrop? If so, what color?

LOLLYPOPS

I play this game with my child clients; I call it the lollypop game. I'm the only one that knows there is a game going on. I do this just to see if the kids are consistent with their choices. I offer him or her a lollypop after their haircut, (parents permission first, of course.) I put two lollypops in my hand, a red one and green one. A boy will pick the green one eight out of ten times, without hesitation. Now it's the girl's turn. I have a choice between a green, orange and a yellow lollypop. The girl will pick yellow eight out of ten times. I really do have a lot of fun with the game. Maybe someday I'll figure out why the outcome is always the same. Which color will you pick when you have your next lollypop?

THE MAN CALLED SAMANTHA

Monday mornings at 10:00 o'clock sharp, a man would enter the salon. His timing was always good since that was not my busy time. He would arrive partially dressed as a woman from his neck down. His blouse and skirt were always colorfully matched and his high heels could actually be flattering with the right choice of pantyhose. We would go through this ritual of questions and answers pertaining to hair colors, styles, manicures, and so on. However, not once, did he receive any services. These visits continued for years. He and I had an understanding that he would always ask me the same questions, knowing he would never buy a service or products. Although I never knew his name, I just called him, "The Man Named Sam".

LITTLE MISSES BIRTHDAY PARTY

I was the first salon in the area to have Little Misses Birthday Parties. They were so much fun for us as well as the girls. Those little princesses were so cute. Their ages ranged from five to twelve years old. We shampooed and styled their hair with very fancy braiding and curls, they received mini-manicures, mini-pedicures, and a mini-make up makeover. I provided balloons and a tiara for the princess. The flashing lights from the cameras and camcorders were running. The parents were having a grand time, along with the birthday girl and guests. After all, she was "Princess for the Day."

HIGHLIGHTING CONFUSION

She certainly was confused about highlighting. The customer, who was a blond, sat in the chair and insisted on having her hair streaked lighter than what she already was. "Let me get this straight" I asked. You are blond, but do not want to be bleached or lightened with color but you want your streaks lighter than your blond hair. Confused? Well, that makes two of us! I explained to her that in order to get lighter streaks I had to use a hair color formula that would lighten her already blond hair. She was still confused. I simply asked her to trust me and let me do what I have to do to get the results that will make her happy. She was still reluctant and confused by allowed me to go ahead anyway. Guess what happened. She got just what she had asked for. Now how did I know that?

FOREVER LATE

She's late! She's always late for her appointment; that is after the deli, getting the hard roll and coffee and stopping at the restroom. Another twenty minutes goes by and she is still in no rush, but at this point, I am. Now my next customers are starting to back up. I soon realize that I need to change her appointments to one half hour later in my appointment book so I can keep on my schedule. Sometimes it's a psychological game we have to play. I love this business.

BLUE AND BLACK BOOTS

As she sat cross-legged in my chair I continued to work on her hair. We were in the middle of a conversation when both of us realized at the same time that one of her shoes was blue with a square buckle and chunky heal and the other was a plain black high heel. We just busted out laughing!! She had wondered why she felt a little off that day! Who knows, she may have started a new fashion trend!

HER MAJESTY THE QUEEN

Every salon has a Queen. That most valued of customers who takes all your time. She is the demanding one, and doesn't care if you are busy with another client or if you have five clients ahead of her. She doesn't care if you are having lunch nor does she care if you can't come to the phone, but when she is trying to make her appointment, you had better answer. She is always late for her appointment and when she finally arrives you have to drop everything for her. When you do get to her, she stalls, saying she has to use the restroom, or she has to tell you a long story or perhaps she needs something to drink After you get her ready to sit under the dryer, she wants her steak and lobster served to her along with her soda all carried on a red velvet pillow. Long live the Queen!

THE RAZOR CUT

After I cut my customers full head of hair with the razor, I had asked her to lift her head back so that I could cut her bangs. Her head went flying up extremely fast and a lot higher than I had expected. Then down came the razor, slicing her nose. Oops! Oops! The haircut would look a lot better without the Band-Aid on her nose.

THE RIP OFF

A sales person walked into the salon with the deal of the century! Against my better judgment I let him talk. He was selling very up-to-date telephones for only twenty dollars each. I tried to dissuade my employees from getting involved with this salesman but I was not influential enough. One of my employees was falling for this deal and decided to purchase two telephones in different colors. The salesman placed two telephones on the desk and she paid him. He disappeared very fast and then she thought she would look at them. Surprise! The boxes were empty. Go figure.

SECURITY DOOR

Eight long hours of drilling, LOUD drilling, all to put in a security door at the salon. The noise after a few hours was becoming unbearable and deafening. When the job was almost complete the law of averages kicked in. The guy drilling the frame of the door slips with his drill, and it goes through the glass. Broken glass was all over the salon and the guy was covered with blood. By now I had a headache from the noise and confusion. I calmly went to the telephone to call the glass company to replace the glass. I had him finish all his drilling on the frame before replacing the glass in fear he would break the glass again. It just goes to show you, it's not over till its over!

THE SMOCK SWITCH

I asked the client to go into the changing room to put on a cutting smock, but when she returned from the changing room she was wearing another customer's shirt, thinking it was a cutting smock. I had asked her politely to quickly return to the room before she was seen wearing the shirt.

THE TANNER

In a high-powered tanning bed, fifteen minutes of tanning was the average tanning time allotted. After the time had passed I heard someone yelling for help through the door, "I'm stuck, I'm stuck! I can't get out of the locked tanning bed!" she yelled. We were lucky that she did not lock the door to the tanning room, so I ran in to help her. I was not strong enough to open the lid of the tanning bed. I told her I was going for help. I would ask the first man I could find. I ran next door and found a gentleman I could ask. He could see that I was concerned so he courteously agreed to help, but first had to ask, "Is she naked?" I replied with a nod and without hesitation he came running to her rescue!

THE UNIFORM

The dreaded uniform! My first job and my employer wanted all of us to look alike. She wanted us to buy the same uniform. The problem with this is that some of us were short or tall, thin or heavy. There was no way we were going to look alike, but we all were forced to buy the same uniforms anyway. The uniforms made us look dumpy and made us feel grumpy. The only one that looked great, of course, was the boss.

UNISEX

The word unisex confuses people. They ask, "Does that mean you cut men's hair?" "What does it mean?" The word means, that men and women can wear the same haircut!

VITAMIN COUNTER

Ever hear about the compulsive customer who counts everything? You know the type of person, the one who purchases a bottle of vitamins along with her exercise program. The vitamin bottle specifies that it contains 100 vitamin tablets. Unfortunately, the manufacturer accidentally put 99 vitamin tablets in that particular bottle. Wouldn't you know that the woman made her husband drive all the way back to the salon, because she felt she was shortchanged for one missing vitamin tablet? The gas alone had cost more for the trip back than the one vitamin was worth.

DON'T DRINK AND DRY

I placed a customer under the hair dryer, knowing that she had a few too many drinks that day. The smell of vodka was very strong on her breath I thought that perhaps she had just come from a long lunch meeting, until I realized it was only 10:00 a.m. After I put rollers into her hair, I knew that the heat from the dryer would affect her one way or another. Within ten minutes, she passed out cold and slid right out from beneath the dryer hood, off the dryer chair, and unto the floor like a wet rag. As I looked around, I noticed a few women trying to contain their laughter; they looked like they were going to explode at any moment. I had to leave my next customer to help the poor woman back into the chair. She was not a small woman, by any means. As I leaned way forward and was trying to lift her dead weight off the floor, suddenly my high heels slipped on the ceramic tile floor. Well down I went, right on top of her! She had no idea I had fallen on top of her. Now, the ladies could no longer hold in their laughter and the room exploded! Their laugher was so loud, that the poor woman, who now is still under me woke up, seeing and hearing everyone laughing! Luckily, she began laughing herself.

MAKE ME LOOK GOOD OR I'LL MAKE YOU LOOK BAD

She just walks into the salon, without an appointment, This customer has no concept of time because it is almost closing time. It's always the same conversation that she needs a shampoo and her hair styled and it is always an emergency. She says this to me twenty minutes before closing (after you have been on your feet for ten hours.) She says," I will leave if you don't have the time to do my hair, I will go home and try to do it myself. (Here comes the old guilt trip!!)" It just gets me every time!" I saw one of her home hairdo's once before, and she looked like a train wreck! I can't take the risk of her doing her hair at home because everyone knows that I do her hair here at the salon. So finally you tell her to please hang up her coat, and drop her shopping bags. Yes, she's been doing her thing all day long and because she can't tell time, you stay longer on the job so that she will look good and that I will look good too!!

NATIONALITIES

I thought you were Jewish, but I thought you were Irish. My employer at the time never asked me and thought I was Irish. I was Irish for the longest time and my Jewish customers thought I was Jewish. One day we were all together in the salon and someone asked me what my nationality was, and I replied I'm Italian, being blue eyed and light in color they all never thought I was Italian. They all laughed, and I was wondering why they were laughing, and than I asked, why are you all laughing? One said I thought you were Jewish, the other person said I thought you were Irish. I said I'm very flexible, and I will be anyone you all want me to be. "I love all people."

KNEE HIGH

She came through the salon door as she was struggling to keep her pants up. I was behind my desk when the woman approached. I got up to introduce myself. As I was coming around the desk, her pants fell lower than her knee highs stockings, (knee highs are the worst looking stockings that are worn only as high as the knees) exposing her quite large panties and her cellulite all through her thighs. She pulled up her pants and followed me to my work area, as we got there her pants fell around her ankles. It seemed to me she was safe with ten to twelve steps after that she lost those pants. I tried not to let her know that I had noticed but by now it was getting quite comical. . Now I had finished with her service, walking out through the door, again for the third time, down come her pants, exposing those knee highs!!!

LATE

"I'm sorry I am late again", she says to you as she is rushing to put her pocketbook down along with her bags, struggling to take off her coat. (If you ever took bets on this person being on time for her appointment you would be rich.) We need a towel that says why we are late! What a list that would be, because I have heard them all. I have learned to make her appointment, one half hour later then she asks for. I know she is wondering why I don't get upset with her, when she comes flying in late. I'll never tell, I just keep smiling!

BEHIND CLOSED DOORS

The salon was all a-buzz!! We were all waiting for the salon's first male waxing customer, who was coming in for a full body wax. (At the time waxing men was all new to us in the salon.) He walked into the salon and he was a very handsome man, as it turns out he later told us he was a male model. He told us he had never had any waxing done and he didn't know what to expect and to be honest neither did we. My waxing technician brought him to the wax room where he would be given a few minutes to change into a robe before she would wax him. Now she entered the wax room and closed the door behind her, so that she could get started waxing him. We all looked at each other, trying to imagine what was going on in that room, and covered our mouths trying not to laugh out loud. We all put our ear to the door trying to listen for any noise, even a yelp, from the wax and hair being removed from his legs. We even tried to climb up on each others shoulders hoping we would hear and even see over the top of the open wall partition(can you picture what this all must have looked like?). He was a real trooper and we never heard a single sound coming out of that waxing room, and let me tell you he had lots of reasons to yell, especially when he was getting a full body wax. A few minutes passed and he came out of the waxing and thanked us for our professionalism. "Does it get any better than this?" What a guy!

WHOSE COAT IS IT ANYWAY

The two coats hung side by side in the closet, same size, same color. (You all know this is a recipe for disaster!!) Well the first customer who was left the salon never had a clue that she left with the wrong coat, and neither did we for a least an hour or more, at which point the second customer decided she was going to leave. Upon buttoning her coat, she reached into her pocket for her keys and pulled out three one hundred dollar bills. She knew in an instant this was not her coat because her coat had only had a car key and a giant ball of Kleenex. I telephoned the previous client and told her that I had her coat along with her money, she was still sure she had her own coat, until I asked her to look in the pockets, of the coat she had, When to her surprise she discovered a giant ball of Kleenex and a car key. The other client kidding remarked to me "seeing as I can't go anywhere with out my car key, do you think I could spend some of this money while I'm waiting?"

I CAN'T HEAR YOU

This person was just nasty and very hard to please. (Not a happy camper.) This particular client wanted a hairstyle she just couldn't have, her hair was much too thin to allow her to have the style she wanted, and she knew it! She demanded I do what she wanted. I tried to be diplomatic and nothing was making her happy! So I finally did what she wanted, and guess what? She hated it! She was yelling at me for everyone to hear through out the salon. I had a brush in my hand and I really felt like I wanted to hit her with it. She grabbed the brush out of my hand and started brushing her hair and swearing under her breath, trying to make me fell bad. I reminded her, that what she asked for in the beginning would not work for her. No way was she going to make me feel bad when she being such a pain. I left her there swearing, to stew in her own soup. Well, it must have worked as she quietly said she would like to talk to me. As I approached her she said very, very softly. I'm sorry. What's that? I can't hear you!! Louder please!, so everyone can hear you, as they did earlier. I'M SORRY she yelled! Everyone in the salon turned to her and said, "We accept your apology!!!"

ODD REQUEST

I didn't quite know how to respond to this customer's request. She said I want you to use the smallest rollers that you have, on my hair today. I said that's fine, and what style would she like when we were finished? (I knew I was going to get very tight curls with these small rollers!) I asked her again, did she want to wear her curly? NO! She replied. I want you to comb out my hair perfectly straight! Please, she said to me "No curls"! What she asked for I knew she was not going to get. What's wrong with this picture? Maybe the size of the rollers!!!

BLUE HAIR

I had two elderly sisters under the dryers, as they watched the new generation of young people with purple, pink, blue and orange hair. The dryers were running and the sisters were talking above the dryer noise, saying if this was my kid, I would never allow them to color their hair these colors, for everyone to hear throughout the salon. Of course everyone in the salon had heard them (We all were laughing). The sisters looked up to see everyone laughing and realized that everyone had heard them talking. I went over to the ladies that were under the dryers, and asked them if they remembered, all the way back to when they were in school and some of their female teachers had blue hair! They both thought for a long moment, and said, yeah! We do remember that, and we all began laughing. Sometimes the generations are not that far apart!!!!!

AUTOMATIC HOUR TIMER

Hustle and bustle in the salon—everyone is busy applying color treatments and perms. The timers are set to go—all timers, of course, are set to different times to go off. Has this ever happened to you? You are thinking it's your timer and have you shampooed or rinsed off your customer's hair? When, in fact, it was not your timer, it was someone else who needed to be rinsed off. Bells' going off all over the salon gets pretty crazy and funny at the same time. Especially when you and your co-workers know what is going on at the time. I always say "do you hear bells; if you do you are falling in love." Ha ha! Be professional and smile and the customer never knows that was not her bell.

BITTER SWEET

My new client was recommended by a dear friend. She was recovering from an illness, which resulted in the loss of her hair, so she had become dependent on a wig. She came into the salon wearing the wig that I have to say looked very natural. Not knowing it was a wig, I was shocked when she pulled the wig off to expose her natural hair. She told me that when her hair grew back in it was totally gray. She previously had done her own hair at home by using a famous name color treatment; however, for whatever reason, her hair turned orange and she came for help. I was able to correct her hair color problem and she went away happy because I freed her from her wig. Thinking back to when I hated to work on wigs, I suddenly realized how important—even essential—a wig can be to a person. So now I'm not sorry for the time I spent styling wigs in the past.

WHAT WOMEN TALK ABOUT

MEN!

Of course we talk about men! It's funny; a new bride will come into the salon full of joy and hope. She is telling us that he is the best in everything and this love will last forever. Now I turn to my other customer and she's bitching about her husband, after seven years of marriage that he was no good and she wants to broom him. The big "D," yep, Divorce. My head is going back and forth between both of them. They had just covered the entire world, men, dating, and babies between two styling chairs. It went from weddings, hope, and fulfillment, with the newlywed to disappointment, despair, and divorce. Oh, now back to dating again. My head was spinning!

KIDS!

I move over to another styling chair, and I am caught up in the world of breast-feeding and teething babies.

RECIPES!

"What will I cook tonight?" she said, while I was getting her ready for her haircut. She was flipping the pages of a food magazine, than another customer said "I don't feel like cooking tonight". All of a sudden she had realized that she did have a very easy chicken dish recipe that she would share with all of us. We all agreed to try this recipe and then compare notes about it at next week's hair appointment.

DIETS!

There isn't a women that doesn't come in the salon who would say "I need to diet" to loose weight. (Just a few pounds or a few inches off my tummy) We were all talking about this weight problem as we were having just one more cookie with our coffee at the salon. "Women just love their sweets!!!"

EXERCISE

Up goes the arms and out go the legs, fifteen minutes of this now I am hungry with all this exercise. It's time for a break and another cookie!

We all talk about the same subjects, "That's Life."

HE SAID SHE SAID

Very early in my career my boss at the time asked if I would stock the shelves on the left side with shampoo. Naturally, I did what she asked me to do. Just as I had finished, her husband walked in the back door and asked me what I was doing. I told him that I put the shampoo up on the left shelve. He said, I would like you to put them on the opposite shelf that was on the right, I said ok, I can do that. Then my boss came back and said oh no, I wanted them on the left shelf, I did look at her kind of surprised and said ok. Now her husband returns for the second time again and says to me, "oh no, I meant the right shelve. Will you please move all of the shampoo over to the right shelf now?" He turned and left the area and I thought something very strange going on here. I decided to stop everything and sat down with my arms crossed. At this point I was totally confused. They finally came to me at the same time, and asked me what was the hold up.

I couldn't stop laughing!! And said the hold up was them! One wanted the left shelf filled with shampoo and the other one wanted the right shelf filled with shampoo. I suggested they talk first and than let me know what they really wanted! They started to laugh after they had realized what they had just put me through. I said "thanks guys."

BODY LANGUAGE

It's amazing how, when you work with someone for a long period of time, you can send messages by making eye contact. One day in the salon, a guy came in, approached the desk and asked if he could have a haircut. He said he had a gift certificate from a friend. A feeling came over me about this guy. I had a gut feeling that he had a weapon in his pocket. I made eye contact with one of my employees, who has been with me for many years, we started "talking" with our eyes and she understood my message. I had a feeling he had a knife! I, myself, started his haircut and kept talking to him to make him feel more comfortable. I did not get the feeling at the time that he would harm me; but I still felt he had a knife. We continued talking and he brought up the subject of weapons and told me that he always traveled with a knife for protection. Talk about body language and gut feelings!

SHAMPOO AND WET HANDS DON'T MIX

Did you ever try to hang on to a greased pig? That's not quite what happened to me, but it was close. In the old days, I really don't want to say how long ago that was, shampoo came into the salon in glass gallon bottles. My job was to fill the smaller bottles with this shampoo for our use. I had finished filling all the small bottles, some of the shampoo flowed on to my hands and now were very slippery. As I lifted both glass gallons to put them away, they both instantly slid off my hands and crashed together like two giant cymbals. I closed together closed my eyes as the glass exploded all around me. My boss said, are you all right? Yes I had replied, but I just couldn't hold on to those slippery pigs!!!!

WET AND WILD

My first week in hairdressing school, is one I will never forget. My Mom graciously agreed to come in to my school to be my first customer, for a shampoo and style. I was so happy to see her there and very excited to get started on her hair. My instructor was guiding me as I started on my Mom's hair. I snapped open a smock and placed it around her neck. I tilted her chair back to make her comfortable and placed her head into the shampoo bowl. Now I was ready for my first shampoo! I was so excited; I turned up the faucet to full pressure. The hose went wild, flying all over the place, and I couldn't catch it. There was water on the ceiling, the walls were dripping and my instructor and Mom were fully soaked. We all looked at each other in amazement, than burst into laughter. What else could we do? Mom was such a good sport, she never mentioned it again, but I never forgot it!!

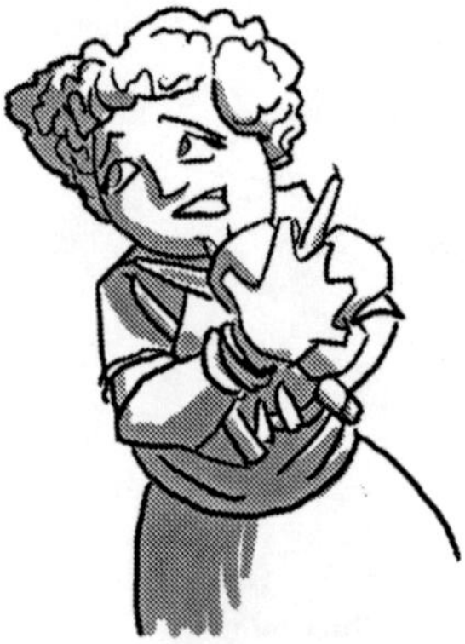

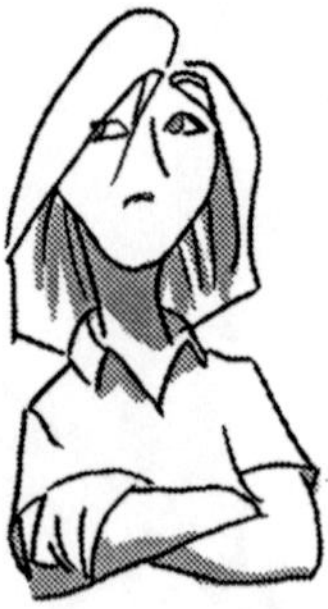

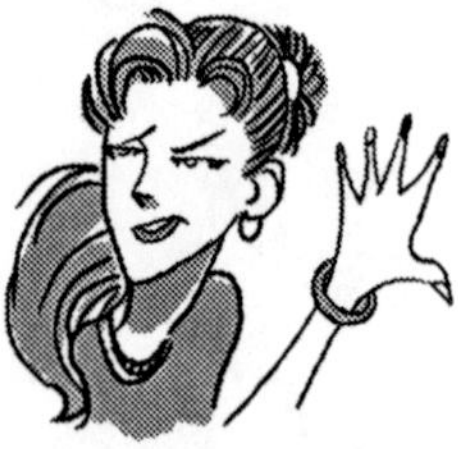

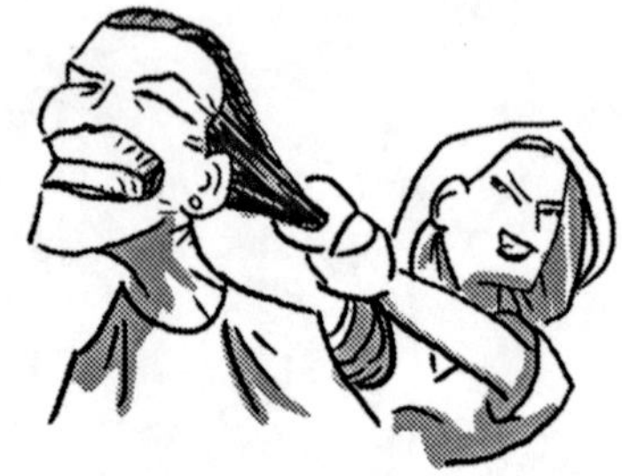

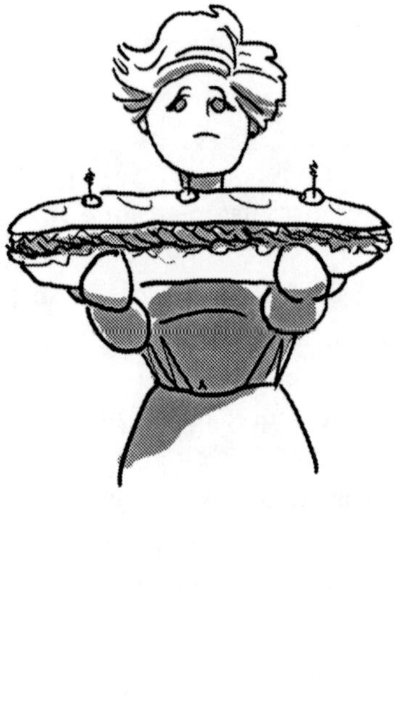

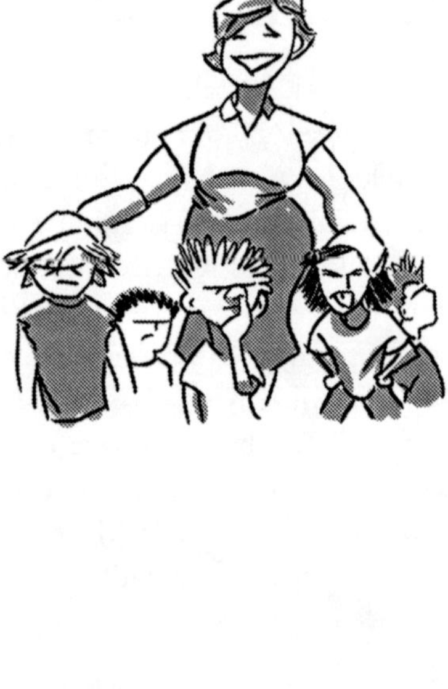

FINAL MEMORABLE BITS AND PIECES:

Giving a $100 bill for services at 9:30 in the morning

Saying "I tipped you, but I'm taking a shampoo ... Is there something wrong with this picture?

Excuses—the weather is always an excuse not to come—it's too cold, it's raining, it's windy, or it's snowing. Every week someone comes up with one of these lame excuses.

A skinny woman walks in, skinny everywhere, but you have to hear all about her big belly. Please!

Then there is the customer who complains about all the money she spends on her hair—week after week, and then tells me she is going gambling weekend after weekend.

"What do I put on first, the conditioner or the styling gel?"

"When do I condition?"

"I don't know what color nail polish I want so put a different color on each nail and I'll decide after I see how they look."

The salon is busy. A walk-in client comes in (we do accommodate walk-ins) and I tell her the wait is ten minutes and she says it is too long to wait. I said "walk in anytime!"

The "bag lady" that fills her own bag with her choice of products

"Work me in ..." They don't care about your other appointments, and they don't want to wait.

"I have curly hair, and I need a style that's good for me. Do you have any good stylists?" Excuse me!

Dark brunette wants to be blonde with a one-step color.

She wants a body wave with no wave.

"Just a bang trim today!"

We close on Saturdays at 3:00 p.m. It's posted in the front window. Invariably someone walks in at 3:00 p.m.

"Do you do a package deal for the family?"

Ten years ago this was a common one: "Do you have any tranquilizers?"

"I told my husband that I spent the weekend on your boat." (Of course I have to laugh because her husband knows that I don't own a boat.)

"I want three shampoos before you style my hair."

"I want a long, LONG, LONG water rinse."

"I want a cold water rinse."

"Do a temporary week rinse, and I want it to last a month."

"Will my perm curl if I get it wet?"

"Cut my hair before my perm so I don't lose my permanent wave."

Exercise machines. "Do these exercise machines really work?"

"I smudged my wet nail polish."

"File my nails long."

Don't you just love the client who rearranges the nail polishes on the display?

She's late for her hair appointment but needs to be out of the salon in 15 minutes.

"I want my hair set tight. I wash my hair once a week."

"I don't want to tell you who recommended your salon."

"Are those brushes clean?"

"I want my hair exactly how you did it last month."

We display a sign that lists all the services we provide and they still ask "Do you cut and style hair?"

"I didn't know the salon was here. How long have you been here?" Sign in window that says "Established 1976."

"Can I use your refrigerator? I just went shopping and I need to put my lunch away."

"You know that stuff you sold me last month. Well, I need some more."

"Cut my hair the same way you did last time."

Split ends, breakage and damaged hair is caused by the leading commercial shampoo advertised on television, but the client believes what she sees on television and she swears by that shampoo!

"This tanning lotion doesn't work."

"I hate that shampoo."

"Conditioners make my hair too soft."

"I want my hair as full as you can get it without teasing or spraying."

"Can I save money on leg wax if I brought in my own candles?"

"Can I save money if I shampoo my own hair?"

"Sorry, I don't have any extra money for your tip."

The client hands you a $100 bill for an $8.00 bottle of shampoo.

"I need a permanent wave, but you have to come pick me up."

God gave you two ears, one for you and one for me …

    Among all of the giggles and moments of frustration and good times, there are lessons to be learned. If I had to pass on a few words of wisdom to the next generation, it would be these: Stay focused. Perseverance and determination will turn you into a pro. There will always be "challenging" customers, mistakes and problems, along with good friends to be made, good times to be had and a lot of laughs to be shared. So, kick butt! With all the crazy things that happen, always keep smiling. You'll get there.

978-0-595-43108-3
0-595-43108-9

Printed in the United States
90021LV00004B/580-660/A